FLIGHT
OF THE
WINDRIDER

WRITTEN AND ILLUSTRATED BY

REAGAN WORD

SCIENCE OF THE SOUL RESEARCH CENTRE

Published by:
G. P. S. Bhalla, Secretary
Science of the Soul Research Centre
c/o Radha Soami Satsang Beas
5 Guru Ravi Dass Marg, Pusa Road
New Delhi 110 005, India

For internet orders, please visit:
www.ScienceoftheSoul.org

For book orders within India, please write to:
Science of the Soul Research Centre
c/o Radha Soami Satsang Beas
BAV Distribution Centre, 5 Guru Ravi Dass Marg
Pusa Road, New Delhi 110 005

Other children's books from the same publisher:
The Journey of the Soul
One Light Many Lamps
A Room Full of Sweets

First edition 2012

19 18 17 16 15 14 13 12   8 7 6 5 4 3 2 1

ISBN 978-93-80077-23-9

Printed in India by: Thomson Press (India) Ltd.

To my Captain,

who taught me how to fly

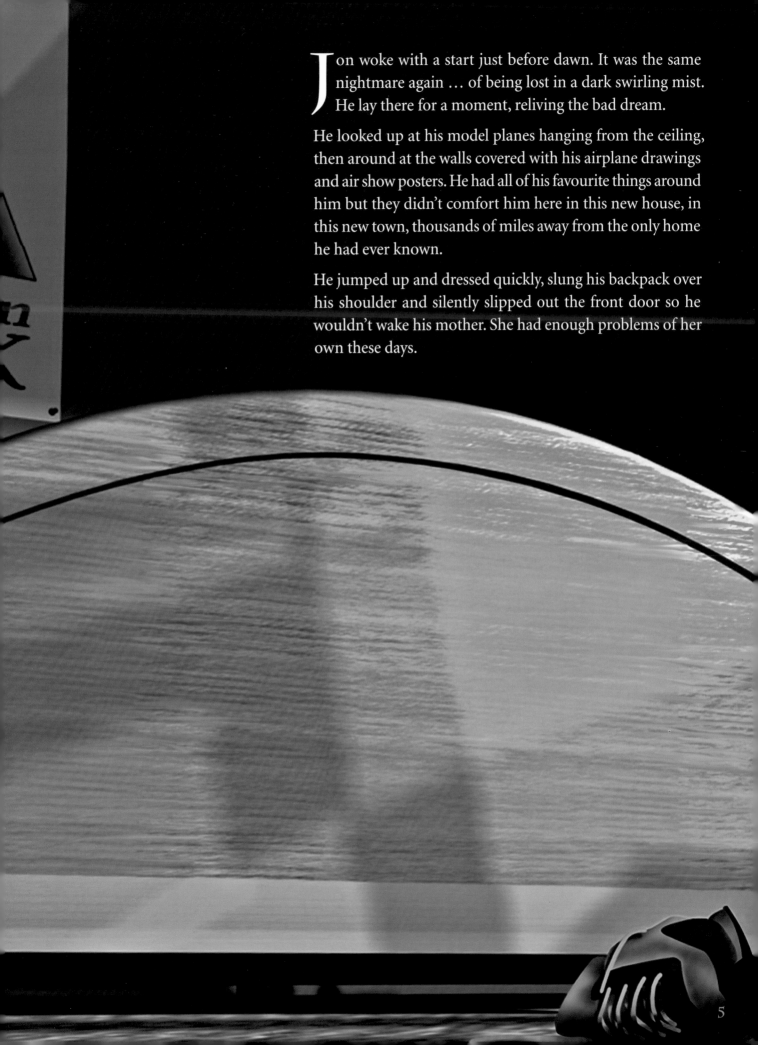

Jon woke with a start just before dawn. It was the same nightmare again … of being lost in a dark swirling mist. He lay there for a moment, reliving the bad dream.

He looked up at his model planes hanging from the ceiling, then around at the walls covered with his airplane drawings and air show posters. He had all of his favourite things around him but they didn't comfort him here in this new house, in this new town, thousands of miles away from the only home he had ever known.

He jumped up and dressed quickly, slung his backpack over his shoulder and silently slipped out the front door so he wouldn't wake his mother. She had enough problems of her own these days.

Daybreak streaked the crystal sky with yellow-orange. Jon swung onto his bike and pedalled off down the street. The crisp morning breeze felt good on his face. Being outside under the open sky instantly cleared his mind. There was only the whirring sound of his spinning bicycle wheels as he pedalled to the main road.

Left turn, then one mile flat out, leaving everything behind. Right at the old hardware store, eight more blocks, then another right at the junkyard with the dusty barking Doberman. Free sailing then for a quarter mile along the back road to the place where the world ends and dreams begin – the airport runway. Breathless, Jon swept through the side gate and pulled over, hoping to see a plane take off.

Luck! A small Cessna taxied out onto the tarmac. Jon watched, enthralled, and at that moment … he was on the plane as it wheeled down the runway, picking up speed, faster and faster, and then … *Liftoff! Airborne! Freedom!* He was flying away, up and up into the yellow-orange sky, away from the new town, away from the new school full of strangers.

When the plane was finally out of sight, Jon pulled out his sketchbook and began working on the drawing of a plane he had started last night. Soon he was flying free again, this time sailing away in a world of crisp lines, subtle shadings and sky blue. At last, he looked up and checked his watch…. *What?! Late for school!* He slid the sketchpad into his backpack and sped off down the road.

Jon tore onto the school grounds, jumped off his bike and dashed to his math class just in time for the second bell. Breathless, he slid into his seat. Mr. Bronson was still writing a long list of problems on the board, so Jon pulled out his airplane sketch to steal a few more minutes of drawing time.

"What's your answer to number five, Jon?" Mr. Bronson asked.

Completely absorbed, Jon heard nothing and kept drawing.

"Hey, earth to Plane Brain. It's your turn," the class bully sneered.

Jon looked up to find Mr. Bronson and the whole class staring at him, waiting for his answer.

"Sorry, what's the question?" Jon stammered, his face flushing beet red.

That afternoon, Jon ran out onto the playground where the soccer captains were choosing their teams. One by one, boys were chosen to play. Jon bit his lip and stared at the ground, praying he wouldn't be the last one to be chosen … yet again.

Finally, the first captain groaned, "Oh, all right, I'll take Jon." Jon's chest tightened. His last ounce of confidence sank into his shoes but he managed a grin and a nod.

It was a rough game. Jon was trying so hard, he kept losing the ball and flubbed an easy goal. Mercifully, the game finally ended.

The other players ignored Jon and walked off together, laughing, joking and horsing around. He headed back to the locker room by himself, reliving his missed goal over and over in his mind.

Discouraged by his rough day at school, Jon wearily pedalled past the airport on his way home. He was hoping to see another plane take off. He pulled over next to the tarmac to wait, took out his sketch and studied it. A sudden gust of wind swept the drawing out of his hand. It floated along until a nearby man snatched it from the air.

"Nice catch!" Jon said.

The man smiled and held up the colourful drawing. "Did you draw this?"

"Yes, sir," Jon answered.

The man studied the page. "The Windrider, eh? Nice design." He looked up at Jon. "What's your name?"

"Jon. They call me Plane Brain at school because I'm always drawing airplanes."

The man nodded and smiled again like he understood.

"I like to draw planes too. My name's Tom Skyler but everybody just calls me Sky, because that's where I like to be most of the time."

"You're a pilot?" Jon asked.

"Yes, I'm the flight instructor here," Sky answered. He looked down at the drawing again. "Who taught you how to draw like this?"

"My dad."

"That's great," Sky said, handing back the sketch.

"It's not so great any more … my dad died last year."

"I'm sorry to hear that," Sky said, studying Jon's face.

"My mom and I just moved here from back East," Jon said softly. He stared at the ground, remembering his father. "Guess I'd better get going," Jon said, not really wanting to leave at all.

Sky extended his hand and gave him a warm smile.

"Not to worry, son. Things can change. Be open. Be ready!"

Struck by the words, Jon shook Sky's hand. But what did they mean? he wondered as he pedalled homeward.

Jon parked his bike and stepped inside the house, relieved to finally be home. His mom's new job kept her working late now, so the house was quiet, empty and dim in the fading light. Jon grabbed a box of cereal from the kitchen, then headed into his room, tossing his backpack into the corner.

The noise woke Tito, his pet gecko, who had been sound asleep in his pickle jar on Jon's desk. Jon sat down and absentmindedly ate cereal out of the box as he stared off, thinking back over his hard day at school. Finally, he looked over at Tito and tapped on the jar.

"You feel lonely here too, don't you, Tito? We just don't fit in."

Tito tilted his bright green head and blinked as if he understood every word.

Trying to shake off his dark mood, Jon grabbed his Windrider sketch and started pencilling in more blue sky. After a few moments, he held up the picture and took a long look. Then, with a sigh, he laid it down again.

"I don't know, Tito. What's the use of making these drawings anymore?"

Jon walked to his dresser and picked up a framed photo of his father and himself at an air show. He ran his finger gently over the smiling faces, remembering, then set the photo back down.

He pulled on a T-shirt and sweat pants and flopped onto his bed. He was sinking deep into the misery of his memories when Sky's words drifted back into his mind. *Things can change. Be open. Be ready.*

"If things *could* change … more than anything else … I would just like to know where I belong now," Jon said softly. Exhausted, he soon fell into a deep sleep.…

A gentle breeze billowed the curtains in Jon's room. He opened his eyes to discover that he was now smaller than a pushpin and standing on his desk next to a real Windrider, complete with pilot. The books on his desk were as tall as skyscrapers.

The pilot smiled a big friendly smile. "Hello. I'm Captain Windsmith. I was asked to deliver this plane to you."

"By whom?!" Jon asked, baffled and amazed.

"By the Architect of Everything and Everyone."

"You know him?!" Jon asked, way beyond impressed.

"Sure do. I've been working for him for years," the Captain said. "That's why I'm here. You're my latest assignment, so you're under my special care."

"Really?" Jon was stunned that the Architect of Everything and Everyone even knew who he was, let alone had such an interest in him. No one else around here seemed to even know he was alive.

"So,… how about this plane?" the Captain said, proudly introducing the Windrider with a dramatic sweep of his hand.

"It looks just like my drawing!" Jon beamed.

"It does indeed. Ready to take her up?"

"Really?!" Jon's eyes shot wide open.

"You bet. That's my job, teaching new pilots like you how to fly. You do want to learn how to fly, don't you?" The Captain asked with a knowing grin on his face.

Speechless, Jon could only nod. He looked closely at the Captain's face. "Hey! You look a lot like Sky."

"Think so? Must be a coincidence," twinkled the Captain.

"Do you really think my Windrider will fly?"

"Looking at your design, I think she'll take to the wind like a champ. That is, if we can get your corn flakes off the runway," the Captain chuckled, tossing Jon a helmet and goggles.

Eager to get going, Jon pulled on the gear and struggled to push a giant flake out of the way. Then he ran to the plane, climbed into the cockpit and listened intently as the Captain talked him through the steps on the checklist for takeoff, one by one.

"OK, fire her up, Jon," instructed Captain Windsmith. The engine roared to life. Jon's heart was beating wildly.

"Give her full throttle forward!" the Captain ordered. Jon firmly pushed the throttle and they taxied down the desktop … faster and faster. With a final lurch, the Windrider lifted off and was in the air.

Jon was ecstatic. But with a stomach-turning drop, the plane suddenly pitched downward, and they were soon skimming along the floor passing bedposts and shoes the size of mountains at breakneck speed.

CELEBRATE FLIGHT!

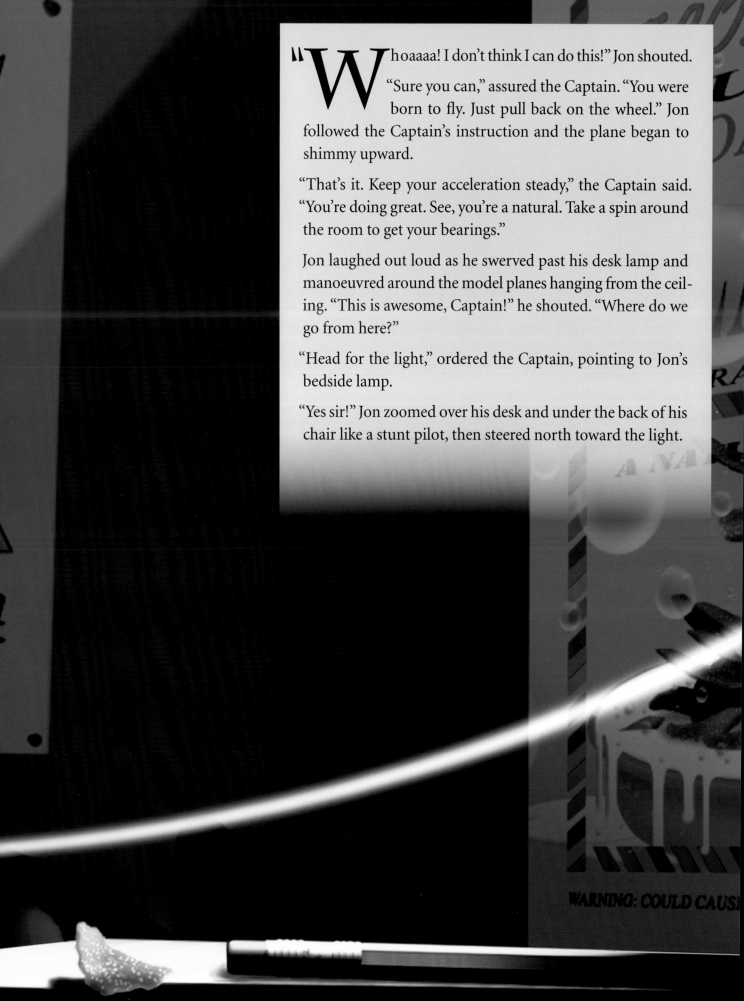

"Whoaaaa! I don't think I can do this!" Jon shouted.

"Sure you can," assured the Captain. "You were born to fly. Just pull back on the wheel." Jon followed the Captain's instruction and the plane began to shimmy upward.

"That's it. Keep your acceleration steady," the Captain said. "You're doing great. See, you're a natural. Take a spin around the room to get your bearings."

Jon laughed out loud as he swerved past his desk lamp and manoeuvred around the model planes hanging from the ceiling. "This is awesome, Captain!" he shouted. "Where do we go from here?"

"Head for the light," ordered the Captain, pointing to Jon's bedside lamp.

"Yes sir!" Jon zoomed over his desk and under the back of his chair like a stunt pilot, then steered north toward the light.

WARNING: COULD CAUS

Pulling the Windrider upward into a steep climb, Jon zipped inside the lampshade and soon they were soaring up through a starry sky. They sailed through a bank of fluffy white clouds lit by a bright full moon.

"Awesome!" shouted Jon, thrilled by the breathtaking panorama all around them. "Where are we?"

"We're in another world. Welcome to inner space!" the Captain said, exuberantly holding up his hands toward the sky.

"Inner space?" Jon asked.

"That's right, Jon. I've been sent here to show you that there is much more to life than what you know on earth. There are many worlds in the creation."

"For real?" Jon asked, fascinated by the Captain's words.

"Absolutely!" beamed the Captain, bursting with enthusiasm. "There are worlds within worlds. Worlds you can't take a plane to. Worlds you can't even take your body to. You have to travel with your mind. And beyond that there's an endless world of brilliant light where only your soul can go."

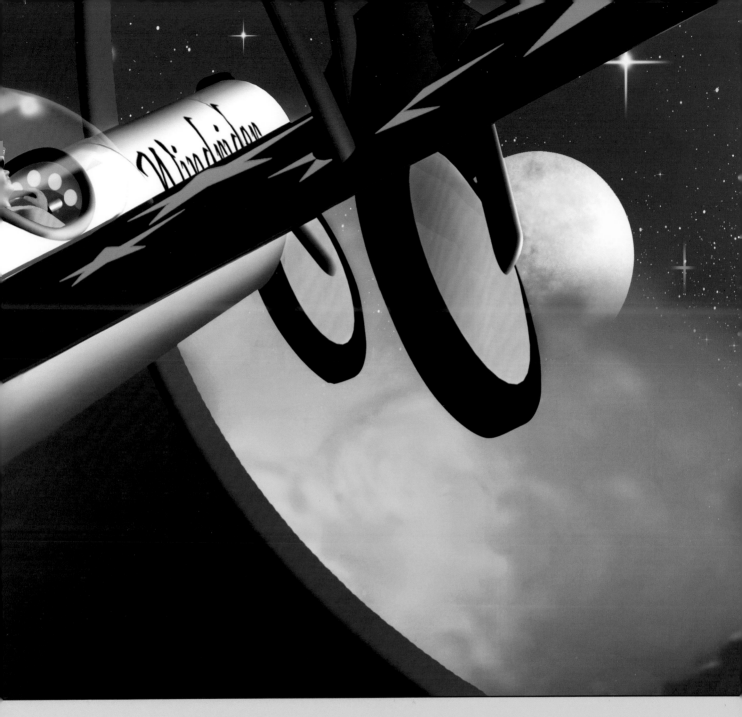

"Really?! But how does the soul get there?" Jon asked, spellbound.

"It catches a ride on a secret, superfast power-stream of sound and light," answered the Captain, having made the journey a thousand times himself.

"Wow! Can I do that?!"

"You sure can, Jon! But that'll come later. First, you need to learn how to pilot your life on earth."

"I don't seem to fit in there too well these days," Jon called back.

"You're a born flyer, son, so you're more at home in the skies," the Captain answered. "Look down to the right. There's nothing like a little altitude to change your attitude…."

Jon looked down at the earth far below them. It looked so tiny and insignificant, floating there in the shoreless sea of stars. From way up here, all his problems there seemed tiny and insignificant too.

"Don't worry, you'll find your way in the world, Jon. You're being guided every step of the way," the Captain reassured him.

Catching a powerful stream of midnight wind, the Windrider climbed higher and higher into the heavens. Jon gazed up at the stars, his heart soaring. He thought about the Captain's words and smiled. It was true. He felt right at home up here in the sky. In fact, this was the most right he had ever felt in his whole life.

Just then, the Windrider sailed into a glittering golden mist and soon a shower of stardust swept all around them.

"Listen to that!" said the Captain, his voice filled with wonder, as the specks of light danced around them, ringing and tinkling in soft musical tones. Jon listened and watched in amazement as the dazzling lights left long glowing trails in every colour of the rainbow.

"What is that sound, Captain?" Jon called back to him, mystified.

Captain Windsmith broke into a bright smile. "It's the Big Secret behind everything, Jon. The Architect of All Things created the whole cosmos, and everything in it, out of sound and light."

"Wow! Really? Even rocks?" Jon asked, amazed, trying to understand.

"Even rocks. A stone is just frozen music, frozen light," the Captain answered, handing Jon a green stone.

Jon looked down at the smooth solid stone in the palm of his hand. It began to glow and vibrate with life, a cluster of twinkling stars forming in its centre. Then it dissolved into a little pool of ringing light and vanished into thin air. Astonished, Jon stared wide-eyed at his empty palm, then looked back at the Captain.

"I have to learn more about this!"

"You will learn many things in time, Jon … many things," the Captain said, smiling to himself.

The Windrider sailed on through the night. Jon spotted a flock of radiant white swans gliding by. He pulled up alongside them, then eased back on the throttle to cruise along with them for a while. He was close enough to hear the beat of their huge graceful wings.

"They're beautiful!" he said in an awed voice. "Where are they going?"

"Home," the Captain said. "Those are special swans. They have their own inner sense that guides them back to where they belong."

"Like a compass?" Jon asked.

"Exactly," replied the Captain.

They are lucky, Jon thought to himself, wishing he could receive some sign that he too would find his way to where he belonged.

The Windrider lifted even higher now. Leaving the swans far below, the plane flew deeper and deeper into infinite inner space. Jon shifted his gaze far into the distance and suddenly gasped. A massive swirling vortex appeared in the indigo sky, revealing a brilliant realm within, swept with pastel colours.

"What is that?" Jon shouted.

"The portal to the beyond," the Captain answered.

"Can we go there?" Jon called back, excited.

"It's not so easy to get through a portal, Jon. It takes a lot of courage and great concentration to break through the sky to the next world."

"I want to try!" Jon said, feeling confident with the Captain behind him.

"Are you sure? It can get pretty rough."

"Yes! I want to see what's there," Jon said eagerly.

"Okay then, tighten your seatbelt and give us full throttle," the Captain ordered. The Windrider picked up speed, streaking toward the glowing gateway.

After an hour of calm air, things began to go terribly wrong. A sudden patch of jarring turbulence wildly tossed them around.

"What's happening?!" Jon called out to the Captain.

"It's only turbulence," the Captain called back. "Just rough air currents. Keep her steady and ride it out."

Jon tried to calm himself and steady the wheel. He looked toward the swirling portal to see massive black clouds rolling in over the opening and racing toward them at frightening speed.

In a moment the portal was no more. A terrible wall of noise began to avalanche in their direction, sounding like the roaring collapse of an entire mountain range.

The Windrider began to rattle and shudder as if it would break apart at the seams. It slammed up and down, tipping steeply side to side. Jon's heart pounded wildly and his body jerked back and forth, fighting against his seatbelt. A spike of fear shot through him.

And worse, the Windrider was now engulfed in the boiling black cloud. Jon could not see one inch past the canopy. A sudden jolt ripped the wheel from his grasp. They spun out of control as a dark power lurking within the cloud began to pull them toward itself.

Suddenly, a serpent the size of a planet reared up from the chaos of churning clouds. It hovered high above the Windrider, whiplashing its tail around the tiny plane.

"Captain! It's got us!" Jon cried out.

"It's not real! It's like your nightmares. It's just your fear looking like something real," the Captain called back.

The serpent grew larger and larger at terrifying speed, instantly dwarfing the plane.

"It's getting bigger!" Jon shrieked.

"It's growing because you're feeding it. You're giving it life. Pull your attention away from it."

"How?!" Jon shouted.

But before he heard the answer, the serpent opened its massive mouth, blacking out the entire sky. With a horrific hissing sound, it sucked them toward its gigantic gaping jaws and razor fangs.

Jon desperately tried to turn the plane but the powerful counter-force torqued the Windrider into a violent barrel roll. They spiralled out of control, spinning round and round, and down and down, deep into the narrowing black throat of the serpent. Jon was frozen with fear, his gaze locked on the black abyss below.

Captain! he called out in his mind, unable to speak or think or move.

"Jon! Look up! Focus on the bright light above us. It's the portal," the Captain instantly called out to him. "Concentrate all your attention on the light, then turn the plane toward where you want to go."

Jon snapped out of his trance. He searched the darkness, straining to find the light of the portal. Then he spun around and saw it.

He concentrated as he never had in his life. With every ounce of his willpower he stared into the light with a laser-like gaze until nothing else existed for him. He saw the light and only the light. It grew bigger and brighter with each moment.

The serpent screamed out as if mortally wounded. Jon wrenched the wheel to the right with all his strength and the Windrider banked into a wide sweeping arc. The shuddering turbulence instantly stopped as the plane shot upward toward the portal. The roaring chaos of sounds died to an unearthly quiet.

But Jon didn't notice. He didn't even notice the serpent slowly vanishing and the black clouds dispersing into the nothingness from which they had come. He only saw the light. He only knew that his fears felt far behind him now, like a bad dream that fades at the break of day.

"Well done, Jon! Well done. You conquered the demon of your fear. You passed the test with flying colours," the Captain said, beaming.

"I wouldn't have known what to do back there, Captain. Thank you for helping me through it," Jon said, his voice filled with gratitude. He smiled to himself. It all seemed so simple now. With the help of the Captain, he had found and focused the laser light of his attention on his goal, and his goal had become his reality. A feeling of peace and calm flooded his being.

The Windrider sailed smoothly into the shimmering portal. The plane caught a powerful current that swept them forward on the crest of a great wave of light. It poured them into a roaring river of radiance and soon they were clear-sailing through a swirling tunnel of starry brilliance. Jon could feel that the Windrider and even his own body no longer seemed to be made of solid material.

In that very moment, they glided into a breath-taking new realm. Jon suddenly felt as if he were floating free, weightless and light as air. He looked around in wonder. Great waterfalls of light were roaring down from somewhere far, far above and cascading to somewhere far, far below.

"Awesome," Jon whispered, barely audible. He was just thinking that he wanted to stay right here in this very spot forever when he looked up ahead and saw it – an immense mountain of light rising up

from a luminous sea of light. Wave upon wave of ringing radiance pulsed rhythmically from the peak. The energy supercharged the entire atmosphere and tingled through every cell of Jon's being, filling him with joy.

Jon felt the pull of the musical light as it flowed back toward the mountain again, like the tide of a great sea. Something inside him wanted to break free and flow with it, let the current carry him all the way to the foot of the mountain. He gazed up at the peak, entranced, enchanted, unable to move.

"I want to go there, Captain," he said softly but with firm resolve. The Captain smiled, remembering the first time he saw the mountain so very long ago.

"Not yet, son," the Captain said, his voice full of warmth and understanding. "When you're given your wings you will go there, and far beyond, to worlds filled with much more wonder than this one."

Full of longing, Jon stared up at the magnificent mountain. He wondered how he could possibly leave and how long it would be before he got his wings and could return. The Captain's voice finally called him back with words Jon did not want to hear....

"It's time to go, Jon."

Jon finally shifted his gaze to the control panel, then banked the Windrider around toward the portal. He looked back one last time, wanting to imprint everything here deep into his being and hold it there forever.

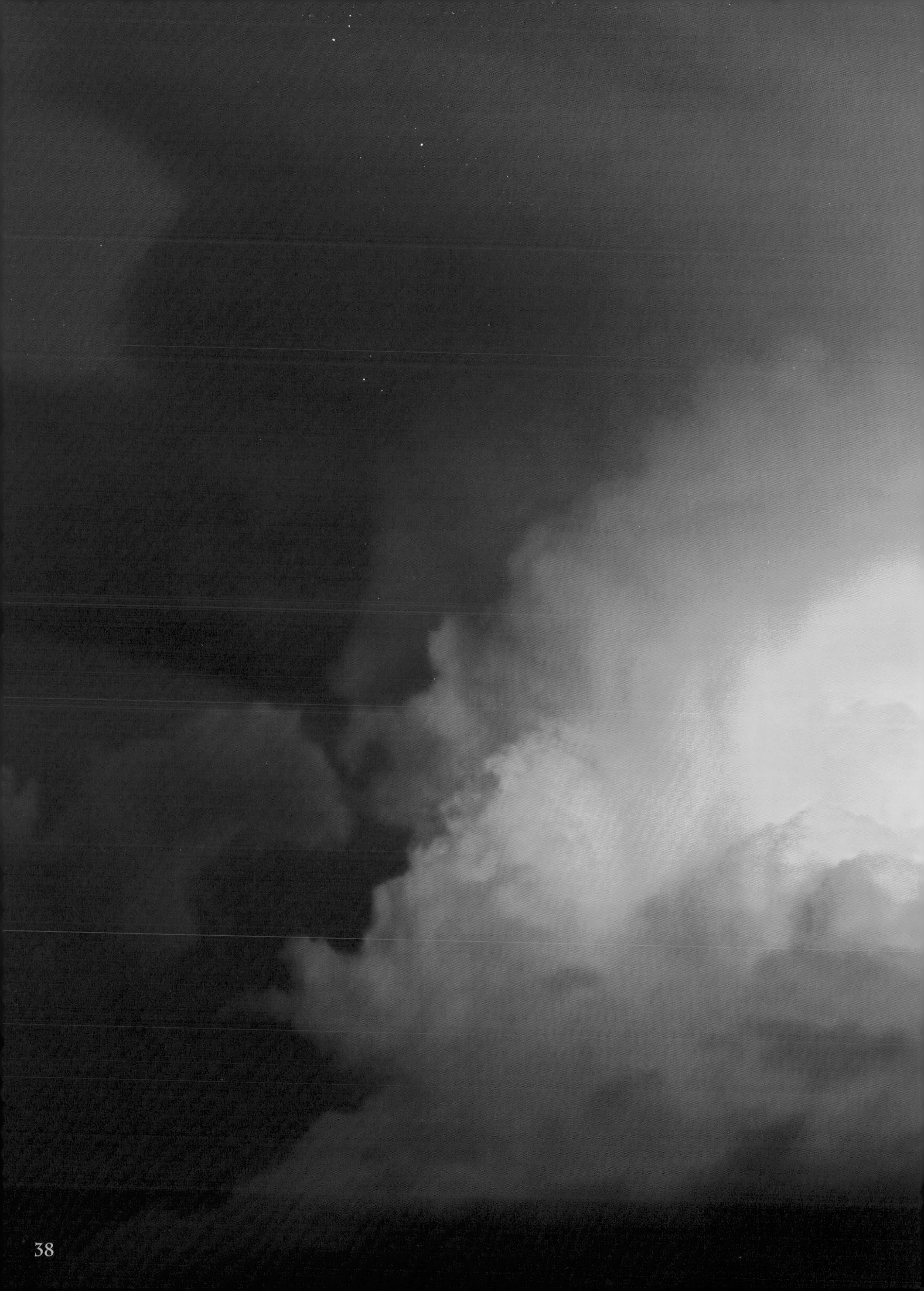

On their journey homeward Jon and the Captain mellowed into a reverent silence as they glided through a golden sunrise. They sat, lost in the wonder and majesty of the timeless moment and all they had just seen.

Finally the Captain broke the silence, for he knew they were nearing the end of their journey.

"She's a real smooth flier, Jon. Your design was just right."

"Thanks, Captain." Jon smiled, feeling a warm glow of confidence wash through his being. "When I get home I'm going to learn all I can about flying. Who cares what people think!"

"That's right. Just be yourself," the Captain answered. "Do what you love to do and do it well. Be the person only you can be."

"I will," Jon said with a newfound determination.

"Prepare for re-entry!" Captain Windsmith ordered, back in pilot mode.

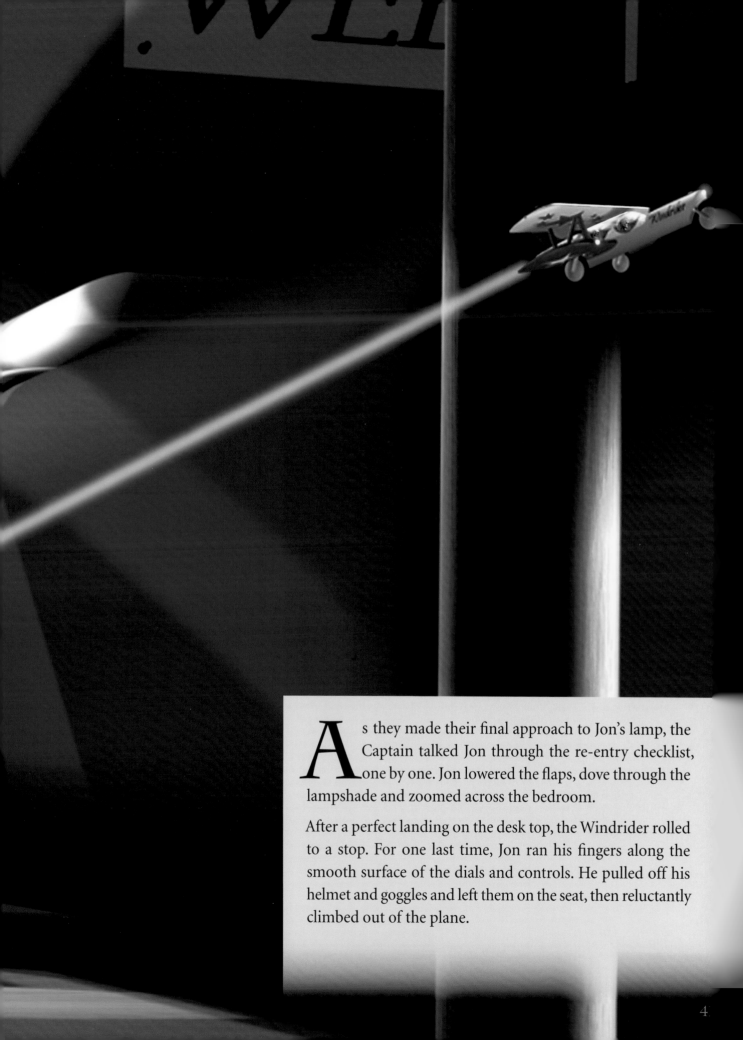

As they made their final approach to Jon's lamp, the Captain talked Jon through the re-entry checklist, one by one. Jon lowered the flaps, dove through the lampshade and zoomed across the bedroom.

After a perfect landing on the desk top, the Windrider rolled to a stop. For one last time, Jon ran his fingers along the smooth surface of the dials and controls. He pulled off his helmet and goggles and left them on the seat, then reluctantly climbed out of the plane.

Captain Windsmith looked into Jon's eyes and gave him a warm smile. He extended his powerful hand. Jon took it with both of his and shook it, never wanting to let go.

"Thanks for everything," Jon said, wishing he could somehow keep the Captain from taking off and leaving him behind.

The Captain knew all too well the turmoil going on inside Jon. He had taken many new pilots on their first flight to the inner worlds. And he had been a first-timer once himself. Re-entry was never easy.

"Here's a little something just for you," the Captain said, pulling an object out of his pocket and pressing it into John's hand.

"Always remember the swans," the Captain said softly. "You have that same homing sense within you, Jon. Listen for it and follow it, and it will lead you to where you belong."

The Captain pulled on his goggles. "By the way, I know Sky could use a little help over at the airport. Why don't you drop by and see him tomorrow?"

Jon nodded, then stepped back as the Captain revved the engine and taxied the Windrider into take-off position.

"One last thing," the Captain called out above the roaring engine. "First Rule of the Road for flyers to the inner realms: keep it to yourself, or they'll be calling you a lot worse things than Plane Brain at school." The Captain grinned and gave Jon a thumbs-up, then took off down the desk runway.

Jon waved a sad good-bye and watched as the plane circled the room, then disappeared into the lamp-shade. He stood there staring into the light for a long time.... Then he looked down at the object in his hand. It was the Captain's compass.

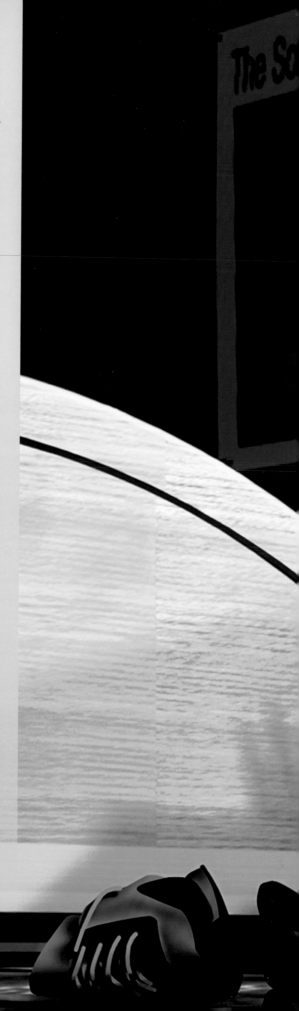

The first rays of sunlight found Jon asleep on his bed and gently woke him with warmth and light. He got up, sat in his window seat and gazed up at the sky. He wanted to remember everything before the noisy day rushed in and swept it all away. Just then, he thought of the compass. Could it be there?

Breathless, he reached up into his shirt pocket, hoping against hope that he would find it there. His fingers brushed against something cool and metallic. He looked down. It was there! It was all true! Memories of his midnight flight flooded into his mind: the Captain, the portal, the mountain of light. It was all real….

He thought about the worlds within worlds and the endless realm of brilliant light where only the soul could go, riding the power-stream of pure energy. It was all still fresh in his mind. He didn't know it then, but it would remain as fresh and new as it was at this moment for the rest of his life.

A gentle breeze brushed the curtain against Jon's arm, and he felt the presence of the Captain. Jon smiled, remembering the warmth and wisdom of the Captain's words. He walked over to his desk and looked down at his Windrider sketch. Then he picked up a pencil and with bold confident strokes titled and signed it. He held the drawing up in front of the photo of his father as if to show it to him, smiled and said, "Just like you taught me, Dad."

Jon looked over at Tito asleep in his pickle jar and lightly tapped on the glass. The little green gecko blinked awake.

"There's more to life than this pickle jar, Tito. Things can change. Be open, be ready," Jon said, gently scooping up his little friend. Jon walked to the window and pushed it open, then set Tito on the branch that brushed against the window sill.

Tito nestled in the leaves for a moment, then ventured a few steps up the branch, ready to explore the amazing new world of the huge tree that reached up toward the sky. From that day on, Jon left his window open and Tito came and went as he pleased.

The Captain was right. Life didn't seem so hard anymore after Jon's midnight flight. He stopped having nightmares and started to find his way in the world. Life was a lot easier knowing that a little altitude can change your attitude, turbulence is only air, and your fears leave as soon as you stop feeding them.

Most days after school you could find Jon at the airport. With Sky's help, he started the Future Flyers Club. Several of his classmates joined him, wanting to learn all about flying like Jon. A few years later, Sky taught them all how to fly.

In time, Jon learned the secret art of flying without wings too. And he learned about the worlds within worlds. One day, Sky gave him a most special and unexpected gift. It was a set of gold wings with a mountain engraved in the middle.

Jon smiled. He knew his real journey was about to begin....